Hello
Is that
Grandma

D0336266

First published in the UK in 2007 by
Alison Green Books
An imprint of Scholastic Children's Books
Euston House, 24 Eversholt Street, London NW1 1DB, UK
A division of Scholastic Ltd
London — New York — Toronto — Sydney — Auckland
Mexico City — New Delhi — Hong Kong

HB 10-digit ISBN: 0 439 95026 0
HB 13-digit ISBN: 978 0 439950 26 8
PB 10-digit ISBN: 0 439 94439 2
PB 13-digit ISBN: 978 0 439944 39 7

Text copyright © 2007 Ian Whybrow
Illustrations copyright © 2007 Deborah Allwright
All rights reserved.

3 5 7 9 8 6 4 2

Printed in China

The right of Ian Whybrow and Deborah Allwright to be identified as the author
and illustrator respectively of this work has been asserted by them in accordance
with the Copyright, Designs and Patents Act, 1988.

For Teddy Traynor, with love from you-know-who — I.W.

For Ben, Isaac and Paloma — D.A.

Ian Whybrow ✪ Deborah Allwright

Hello!
Is that
Grandma?

ALISON GREEN BOOKS

Teddy
phoned
a number.

He went ...

bee-bee-
bee-bah-
beep!

"Hello? Is that Grandma?"

"I can't talk now, Teddy!

I've got my knitting in a knot.

Baaa! Goodbye!"

"Wrong number! This is Sheep.

He dialled **another** number.
He went . . .

Teddy had **another** go.

"Wrong number!
This is Duck.

One-two,

one-two,

one-two.

"Can I speak to Grandma, please?"

"I'm having trouble with my trifle!

MoOOO!
Goodbye!"

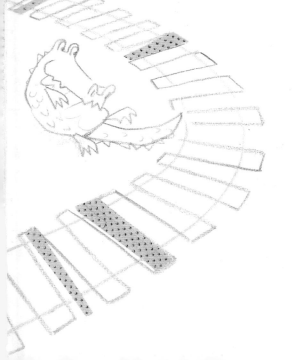

"Those animals are busy!"
Teddy thought. "I wonder why?

"I'd better ask my grandma."
And he gave her another try.

This time Teddy's finger
Went . . .

tip-tap

tip-tap
tap!

"Hello? Is my grandma there?"

"How **delightful** to talk to you, Teddy!"
said the crocodile.
"**Do** come over.

"It's time I had you for **tea**."

"A crocodile!" cried Teddy.

"Help! What shall I do?"

Then the phone went,

preeeep

preeeep ...

"Hello, Teddy?
Is that **you**?"

"Good!" said Grandma.
"Come on round
And have some
birthday tea!"

"I'd **love** to come," said Teddy.
"But will **crocodile** come, too?"

"He's not invited," Grandma said.
"There'll just be me and you . . .

"Oh, **there** you are!" laughed Teddy.
"Yes, Grandma, this is me!"

"And your mum, of course,
and three nice friends . . .

"They're on their way already.
I can hear them knocking now."

When Grandma blew
her candles out,

to Grandma
love
Duck x

"That's Sheep, and Duck and Cow.

Everybody went

clap   clap!

...except that
naughty crocodile.

And the crocodile went,

"Do help yourselves!" said Grandma,

"But when you eat your food,

to Grandma love Duck x

"No phoning at the table, please,

Because that's . . .